Undying Romance

Part 2

'Anna, you have been sick every morning for the past four days,' Penny said. 'I'm arranging to see a doctor to find out what's wrong, and besides, you haven't been eating much.'
In the mornings after the funeral, my mind would always race back to the calendar Carter and I made. We would mark off each day, symbolising one day closer to the wedding, our wedding.
'Tomorrow you are going to see the doctor and you need to get a tonic to get you to start eating again. You have been losing some weight and it isn't healthy,' Penny said, concerned.
Sitting in the doctor's surgery, I felt I was going to pass out. My name was called – 'Could Anna Brown come to room three please.'
'Let's go,' Penny said, as we made our way to the doctor's room.
I truly didn't even know why I was there. My mind just kept drifting to Carter. Penny began to explain everything to the doctor, and within seconds the doctor was arranging for me to have blood tests.
'I would like you to take a pregnancy test, Anna,' the doctor said.
I thought I was hearing things. 'A pregnancy test? Why?' I cried.
'Well, I cannot prescribe anything to help you sleep until I have carried out some tests,' He said.
I did as the doctor asked and returned home. I attempted to eat dinner, got a hot bath and was in bed for 9pm. It was yet another long and awful day.

I awoke the next morning, hardly believing I slept throughout the night. I failed to notice how totally exhausted I was. This was the first time since Carter

had died that I had actually slept properly. I heard Penny in the kitchen preparing breakfast.
As I walked into the kitchen, I was greeted with the overwhelming aroma of coffee.
'Now then, Anna,' Penny said. 'I have made some coffee and toast for you, and I would be happy if I saw you eat it. Remember you have got to telephone the doctor later in the afternoon to get your results. Would you like to go out shopping today, Anna?' Penny continued. 'It would help you to get out of the cottage for a few hours.'
I agreed to go with Penny and got myself ready to go into the city. Just moments before we left, the phone rang. 'Please, Penny,' I asked, 'would you mind answering the phone?'
Again, I was just not in the mood to chat to anyone.
'Anna, I think you should take this call. It's your doctor, and he would like to speak to you,' Penny said, as she handed the phone to me.
'Good morning, Anna!' the cheery doctor voiced on the other end of the line. 'The results of your tests are in and I am pleased to tell you that everything is fine.'
I sighed, a sigh of relief, and was preparing myself to hang up the phone to leave with Penny.
'Also, the even better news, Anna,' the doctor continued, 'you are pregnant and I would like to make an appointment for you, to attend the antenatal clinic early next week.'
'I'm sorry, but could you repeat that, please?' I said bluntly.
'Anna, you're pregnant!' the doctor said, nearly shouting in my ear, responding to my request.
My entire body went numb. I could not speak.
'Anna, are you alright?' Penny asked, somewhat concerned.

'Yes, Penny, I am fine. I am going to have Carter's baby,' I cried.
I couldn't continue the conversation with my doctor, and so Penny took the phone out of my shaking palms and wrote down the time and date of my appointments.
'Oh Anna, I am so overjoyed for you! Come and sit down,' Penny squealed, as she hung up the phone. Penny was in a fluster, jumping up and down. I knew Carter would never leave me.
'I'm going to have his baby.' These were the only words I can manage to say to my ecstatic best friend. I was so filled with joy as I sat with my hands upon my tummy. I was so happy to have been given the time I had with Carter. He won't ever be far away from me.
'Would you mind if we didn't go into the city today?' I asked Penny. To which she replied that she didn't mind at all.
'I don't want to say to Madison or any of the guys at the office just yet,' I told Penny. I wanted to wait until I had my first appointment at the clinic.

I was three months pregnant when I decided to return to work. Everyone was fantastic and totally overjoyed about my pregnancy announcement. Zara stood with her eyes full of tears, and said, 'Oh, Anna, I am so happy to see you and overjoyed about your pregnancy.'
'Thank you, Zara,' I said. 'I am happy to be back to the office again.'
Nothing much had changed at work. We were all a happy team as usual.
'How are things with you and Connor?' I asked Zara.
'Everything is fine,' she replied.

I knew she wasn't going to say how happy they both were, because she didn't want to mention anything that she thought would upset me by reminding me of Carter.
'Zara, please don't hold back,' I said. 'I truly want to know how you and Connor are getting along. I will never forget Carter and I am so overjoyed to be having his baby.'

The months were passing by so quickly. I couldn't believe it. I would be going on maternity leave soon.
'Hi Anna.' Once again I heard that very happy voice (Madison) bounce across the office. 'You are looking very well and may I add, it won't be long until the baby arrives.'
'Penny and I are going to cook a meal at the cottage on Saturday night,' I replied. 'We would love you to come and join us.'
'I would like that,' Madison replied, with that glowing smile.
'Great. See you around seven then?' I sealed the date.
I couldn't wait to get home from the office to tell Penny that Madison would be joining us at the weekend for dinner. I could tell that Penny liked him, but just didn't know how much she *really* liked him.
Penny had decorated the spare room that was once mine as a child when I was growing up in the cottage, and turned it into a beautiful nursery for the baby. As I stood gazing into the room, it made me think of my childhood and parents once again. I can recall the very first day I started to write. It was right here, in this very room. 'This cottage had such beautiful memories, Penny,' I said as I stood gazing, in a daydream.'
'Yes, and many more to come, Anna!' Penny replied.

Just as Penny was adding the finishing touches to the table, I heard Madison's car. As I opened the door to greet him, I noticed he had the most beautiful bunch of white lilies in his hand.
'Anna,' he said, 'I hope you don't mind, but I bought you just a little something.'
As the three of us were seated at the table, we found ourselves having a good old laugh about how we had become friends. 'When will you be taking your maternity leave from work, Anna?' Madison asked.
'In the next week or two,' I replied. 'I can't wait until the baby is born! I would love you and Penny to be the god parents of our baby.'
Both of my friends replied telling me they would be honoured to be the godparents of my and Carter's child. I had asked Rose to make the robe for the christening, and I had already asked Penny to be there for the birth, and she said she would be glad to be there. There were just so many things to think about, and I was both nervous and excited about the experience I was about to endure.
I watched Madison and Penny, as they were engrossed in conversation. They both got along very well. I noticed Penny blush a few times as Madison caught her watching him.
'My goodness,' Madison said, 'it's nearly eleven. I should be on my way now! I would like to thank you both for such a beautiful meal.'
Penny and I both replied that he was very welcome and saw him to the door. After Madison had left, I watched as Penny started to tidy up. 'Anna,' Penny said in a low voice, 'Madison sure is a super guy and he will be a fantastic godfather.' I agreed with her, yawning.
'Can you please go to bed, Anna. You must be very tired. I will go prepare the sofa bed and then when

I go to bed I won't disturb you.' Penny said as she made her way to the bedroom.
As I tucked myself up in bed, I removed Carter's photograph from under my pillow. I placed upon my bedside table a picture of the man that was *My Everything*. I always felt he was with me as I slept.
'Good night, my darling.' I said, as I did every night before I closed my eyes.

The following morning I awoke shortly after 7am. I looked again into the nursery. It looked so beautiful and bright. I looked towards the window in the room and it was there Penny had placed my dear father's rocking chair. She had painted it white. It was beautiful. The white bear that Carter had bought me just weeks before he died was sitting on it.
I returned to my bedroom and Penny was fast asleep. I didn't want to wake her and so I got my pen and paper, made my way to the living room and began to write like I used to.
'Is that the time, Anna?' I could hear Penny shout from the bedroom.
'Yes,' I said. 'It has just gone 9.20am.'
'Why are you up so early, Anna? Did you sleep well?' Penny asked, seemingly worried, as always.
'Yes, Penny, I had a good sleep, but I have decided to do some writing today.'
After breakfast, both Penny and I went down into the village store. It was there that I began to know Natalie. I would go into the store at least twice a week. Natalie and I had become very good friends. Most evenings Natalie worked in the store, which belonged to her parents, whom I had known for many years.
As Penny and I entered the store, we were greeted by Natalie.

'Hello Anna!' she said with a beautiful smile. 'How are you keeping?'
As we chatted for a few minutes, Natalie said 'Anna, I hope you don't mind me saying, but whenever you decide to go back to work after the baby is born, I would be happy to take care of the baby for you. It was always one of my ambitions to become a child minder and now that I am, I would love to be of any help to you!'
'Thank you!' I replied. 'I would like you to be my child minder. We can have a chat one evening and make some arrangements!'

I knew if Carter were alive, he would be happy that I had chosen Natalie to take care of our baby. Natalie was no stranger. I had known both her and her family for a number of years. To be honest, I was thrilled when Natalie offered to take care of my baby. I couldn't think of a more suited person, whom I could trust. I had planned to come out on maternity leave at the end of November, as the baby was due in January. Already, Penny was making arrangements for Christmas. As we were walking through the village, she said, 'Now then, next week, you and I shall go into the city to get some Christmas decorations for the sycamore tree.'
This was the tree Penny and I had planted many years ago, when we were little girls. Every year we would decorate the tree with lots of fairy lights and coloured tinsel, because it meant so much to us.
'I have asked Madison to join you and me for Christmas dinner,' I said to Penny.
She blushed and said, 'Oh, that'll be nice!'

My last day at the office was oh so very busy. 'I am really going to miss you,' I said to Zara as she gave

me a hug. 'Now come on, I'm only going on leave. I will be back in no time at all,' I continued, as Zara sobbed softly.
Just as I was clearing up my desk, I heard Madison's voice, as I looked at him I saw the most beautiful bouquet of flowers in his arms.
'On behalf of myself, and all the guys at the office, we would like to give you this small token!' Madison said. My eyes filled up with tears as I said 'Thank you, thank you all for just being here for me. I will be keeping in touch with you all, this I promise.'
Joe, our boss, then arrived just as I was about to leave.
'Now then, Anna,' he said. 'I want you to call me if there is anything you need, and don't forget, you did say you would pop in and see us from time to time, but only when you can! I'll never forget the first time I met you, Anna,' my boss continued. 'You were sitting at the end of my desk, so excited to finally be getting your first job, sitting beside your dear father.'
All the memories came flooding back to me at once and I began to feel somewhat emotional, after all, it was an emotional day.

Madison walked me out to my car and placed the flowers in the back seats. I gave him a lasting hug and told him I would call after dinner. Driving home I felt so alone. I was going to miss my work a lot, but soon things would dramatically change once my baby was born. I was going to keep myself busy in the cottage by writing, and in the evenings I would have Penny and Natalie over for a chat.

Once I got to the cottage, I arranged the flowers into a vase and then Penny pulled up outside.

'Wow,' Penny said as she came into the cottage. 'What a beautiful bouquet of flowers. Who got you these?' I brushed away a silent tear from my eye as I stood looking at the flowers.
I didn't realise Penny had caught the slight tears falling down my cheeks.
'Now come on, Anna. Let's get changed and go out for something to eat. Why don't we ask Madison too?'
Then I remembered I had forgotten to telephone Madison. 'Yes I will ask him now!' I said, as I hurried to the phone.

We arrived at the restaurant shortly after 8pm. Madison was already there.
'Hi girls,' he said, as he showed us to our table. 'It was really nice of you both to ask me to join you tonight.'
'You're very welcome,' I replied.
We had a lovely meal and a good chat about what I will be doing with my time now that I am on leave. I was saying that I was going to be keeping myself busy around the cottage, and that I had also promised Rose I would call into her shop and see her from time to time and of course, I shall be doing lots of writing. Also, I will be cooking dinner every night for Penny, so she won't have to worry about cooking after she comes home from work. Plus, I owed it to her for staying in the cottage to look after me!
'Anna!' Penny exclaimed. 'You really don't have to do that!'
'No, I insist,' I said. 'I owe it to you, and that's what friends are for!'
I watched as both of my close friends chatted to each other and just thought to myself, as I always did,

about how much they were suited to each other, the perfect couple.

Penny and I arrived home at 10.30pm.
'That was a lovely evening,' I said. 'I am glad we went out after all. It really picked me up.'
I kept myself busy over the weeks ahead and before I knew it, Christmas had come and gone in no time. Penny, Madison and I had dinner on Christmas day and chatted most of the night. Natalie spent Christmas evening with us also. That night was the happiest I had felt since Carter passed away. It was now just weeks to go until my baby was due. I just couldn't wait.
On Boxing Day I started sorting my things that I would be taking to the hospital. I packed some baby gowns, and I couldn't help fighting back the tears as I placed them into my suitcase. I picked up Carter's photograph and held it close to my chest, thinking back on all the beautiful memories. Quickly I pulled myself together as I heard the telephone ring.
'Hi, Anna, I hope I'm not disturbing you,' the voice on the other end of the line said.
'Joe!' I exclaimed. 'What a surprise!'
'Everyone at the office said you had called in a few times, but unfortunately I kept missing you,' he laughed. 'I hope you're resting and taking it easy.'
'I sure am. Just another few weeks to go to my due date and I am more excited than anything,' I said.
'You sound great,' Joe said. To which I replied, 'I must admit I am feeling much more like myself. I was sad when I left the office. I had a lot of time on my hands and a lot of time to reflect on the past few months. I think it helped me come to terms with everything, and in no time at all I will be back!'

'You take care, Anna,' Joe said. 'And I shall see you after the baby is born!'
As I put down the telephone, I heard someone at the door.
'Hi Natalie,' I said as I opened the door, 'what a lovely surprise.'
'Well, Anna, I just wanted to pop in to see if you needed anything.'
'Thank you, Natalie. I could do with a coffee and a chat,' I said.
'Would you like to go out for some lunch?' Natalie asked.
'Now I would love that. Would you mind if I called in to see Rose at her shop? I am busting to see the christening gown she has made for the baby!'
We both had a lovely lunch at a beautiful hotel down in the city. Then we went to visit Rose for a short while. I arrived back at the cottage around 4.30pm, and I felt myself getting tired.
'Thank you, for such a nice day!' I said to Natalie. I then went and rested before Penny came home from work.

I awoke to the sound of Penny's voice calling me. 'I am in the bedroom!' I replied. As Penny entered the room, I said, 'my goodness, I am sorry, Penny! I had fallen into a deep sleep and didn't realise the time.'
'Don't worry Anna. Please don't get up, Penny said. I am going to go heat some soup for us. I had a big lunch and so I am not really that hungry. How was your day?'
'Natalie called and took me into the city for some lunch. Then we called in to see Rose at her shop. We had a really nice day and Natalie took her car so I didn't have to drive. I am going to have a bath and

then we can have a proper chat before I retire to bed again! I'm just so tired,' I replied.
I couldn't keep my eyes open, and so around 9pm, I went back to bed. Penny said goodnight and went back to her own house as she had some ironing to do, and told me she would call me from her work tomorrow.

The following morning, I woke up shortly after 8am. I felt a few pains in my lower back, but took no notice of it. After I had some breakfast, I pottered around the cottage, but for some reason I just couldn't settle. I tried to do some writing, but as the hours passed, my pains were beginning to get stronger. I didn't want to alarm Penny by phoning her at work. So I thought I would give Natalie a quick call. The thought crossed my mind that I could be heading towards labour. I knew this was a symptom, but just left it for a while.
'Hi Natalie, I was wondering if you would like to call in and see me if you aren't busy?' I said.
'Yes, sure I will. Just give me about half an hour and I will be there. Are you alright, Anna?' Natalie replied.
'To be perfectly honest, I'm not sure', I said to Natalie. 'I have been having some pains in my lower back since I woke up this morning.'
'Phone the hospital, Anna! I will be with you in no time,' Natalie said, seemingly worried.

I telephoned the maternity unit in the hospital and informed them of my *discomfort*. I was then advised to go to the hospital as soon as I could. Within ten minutes, Natalie was here at the cottage and off we went. On arrival to the hospital, I was greeted by a very pleasant and polite nurse.

‘Hi, my name is Anna Brown,’ I said, with slight pain in my voice.
‘Yes, Anna, it was me you were talking to on the phone. We were expecting you,’ she said as she introduced herself as Charlotte.
‘Let me take your case, and once you have settled into the delivery suite we will get the doctor to come and see you,’ Charlotte said as she led me through two sets of double doors. The nerves were racing throughout my entire body. I was trying so hard to be calm. I knew this wasn’t good for me, or the baby. Natalie took a seat in the waiting area until she was allowed to come in and see me. A short time after I was admitted, the *gyne consultant* came and had a chat with me.
‘Hello, Anna!’ he said. ‘My name is Doctor Bradley, and I would like to ask you a few questions, do a routine check-up, and then we will know what stage of labour you are at.’
After my examination, Doctor Bradley informed me that I was in the early stages of labour, and I still had a while to go before the baby would arrive.
‘Just try and relax, Anna. You are in good hands, and if there is anything you need, please ask. You are very anxious, understandably, but trust me, all will be well,’ Doctor Bradley said as he was heading out the door.
Natalie was allowed to spend a short while with me before she had to go.
‘I phoned Penny to tell her you had been admitted. So she should be here soon. You try and get some rest now, Anna. Penny is going to keep me informed and let me know when the baby is born.’ Natalie said before she left.

I tried to rest, but to no avail as my pains were worsening and worsening.
Charlotte gave me some pain relief, but it just seemed to take the edge off the pains a little. I walked around the ward for what felt like a lifetime.
'*Oh Carter*,' I whispered. '*I wish you were here with me.*' Although, I knew in my heart he was there, in spirit.
Just as I lay myself on top of the bed, I heard voices in the corridor. I heard Penny say, 'Please, could you just tell me which room Anna Brown is in!'
As Charlotte let Penny into my room, I could hear the nerves in her voice - 'Oh Anna, I have been so worried about you. I am so sorry I couldn't get here sooner!'
I introduced Penny to my midwife, Charlotte. Charlotte smiled and said, 'I don't know which one of you is most anxious.'
'Forgive me,' Penny said. 'I have been trying to get here as soon as I could!'
'Calm down, Penny!' I said. 'You are here now and I am very grateful to have you here.'
Charlotte explained to Penny that it would still be a while before the birth, and that she was very welcome to be present as long as it goes according to plan.

I was drifting in and out of consciousness as the pain relief was now making me drowsy. Around 9pm, Charlotte told me she was going off duty and introduced me to the night nurse who would be looking after me throughout the rest of the night.
'Hi, Anna,' the new nurse said. 'My name is Beth, pleased to meet you.'
By 1am I was in my final stage of labour, much to my surprise, and I felt totally drained. Beth was

guiding me through my breathing exercises and I felt a few moments of relief in between my pushing pains. My labour was very, very long, and shortly after 5am, Dr Bradley arrived to help deliver my baby.
'You have a beautiful baby boy, Anna!' Doctor Bradley announced about half an hour later. My baby was then placed into my arms. I looked at him and placed a soft kiss on his little head. I was speechless. He was the image of his Dad. Penny was standing beside my bed, the tears rolling down her face. I had been thinking about some names over the past few months, and *Charlie* really stuck. When I looked at my child *Charlie* was all I could think of, and I knew Carter would have liked it.
'Oh, Anna,' she said. 'He is so much like...' She stopped talking.
'Don't worry,' I said to my friend. 'I truly did feel Carter's presence with me as our son came into this world.'

'I'm just going to weigh the baby now, Anna, and the doctor has to do a routine check,' Beth said as she came and took my little baby. He was crying as Beth placed him on the scales to check his weight. '8lb 2oz,' she said as she lifted him up again. 'You have got a healthy little baby,' she said with a smile.
Dr Bradley then came in again to do the check up on my baby. He congratulated me again. Then Beth handed him Charlie and informed the doctor of my little boy's name.
'Well Anna, young Charlie has got a very strong pair of lungs on him,' Dr Bradley said, as he set Charlie gently back in my arms.

Dr Bradley then headed for the door, along with Beth, and told me they would be back later to check on me before they went off duty.

Penny left the hospital at around 7.30am, and I was then alone with little Charlie. Penny told me before she left that she would let Madison, the guys at the office, and Natalie know about the safe arrival. Charlie fell asleep after I fed him, and so I put him back in his cot and went to sleep myself. I was exhausted. I awoke to the sound of all the babies crying.
'My goodness, Anna,' Charlotte said, standing at my bedside. 'First let me congratulate you, and I must say you have a lot of friends. There have been so many people phoning the ward to ask about you and Charlic!'
I couldn't take my eyes off Charlie. He was just perfect. My life had changed, from the moment he was placed into my arms. Visitors began to arrive at 2.30pm, and of course my good friends Penny and Madison were among them.
'Well done, Anna!' Madison said. 'He sure is a big boy.'
I laughed. 'Yes, 8lb 2oz.'
'Please may I hold him?' he asked.
Still feeling tired from the long labour. I was glad to see my friends, and yet I just wanted to be alone with my son. I remained in hospital for four days and then I was allowed to go home. As I was leaving the hospital I asked Penny would she mind asking Zara and the other guys from the office if they could give me a few days to settle in at home before they come and see us.

'That has already been taken care of,' Penny replied. It was Zara who had told Penny to let me know she would see me later that week.

Everything was just so perfect at the cottage, and Charlie was getting more and more beautiful every day. So why was I so lonely and always tearful?
'It's just you and me,' I would say to my little baby, as his big brown eyes seemed to roam around the room. On the last day of my midwifery visits, I told Charlotte how I was feeling, and that I just didn't know why I was feeling like this.
'You are just going through the *baby blues*, as they are called, Anna. Don't worry. I will arrange an appointment for you to say the GP,' Charlotte said.

Charlie was just over a week old when all my friends from the office came to visit us. I must say, I was glad to see them. They brought beautiful gifts for Charlie, and Zara just wanted to cuddle him all day. Madison was fantastic. He did the shopping and just helped me in every way he could. Joe arrived to visit me the following Sunday.
'I hope you don't mind me calling, Anna, but I just couldn't stay away any longer! I brought the baby a little something!' Joe said as he came into the cottage. Joe had brought a big blue teddy bear, with '*Charlie*' stitched across its chest. The bear reminded me of the one Carter had bought me before he died. It brought chills to my skin.
'I am sure you are very proud of Charlie,' Joe said. 'He is a beautiful baby, and I hope you are resting whenever you get the chance. '
I explained to Joe that I had been resting as much as possible, and Penny and Madison came most days and evenings after work to help out. Joe gave a little

smile and then said, 'Madison is a great guy, Anna, and I know you have both been friends for a long time now. You know Anna,' he continued, 'Madison is so fond of you, and to be honest, he never stops talking about you and Charlie.'
'Yes,' I replied, 'Madison sure is a great guy, and to tell you the truth, one day I hope he meets a nice girl, maybe a girl like Penny.'
As Joe was leaving, I called after him, 'Don't forget, the christening is next Sunday, and you are welcome to come along!'

I loved being at home with Charlie. He was a very content baby, and all I wanted to do was cradle him, every second of every day. I didn't want to put him into his room until he was a few months old. So his crib sat beside my bed. In the evenings before I lay Charlie in the crib, I would sit in the rocking chair and sing a lullaby to him. Those big eyes would look up at me, before he drifted off to sleep. Natalie would call in once or twice a week and bring me some lunch, and while Charlie was sleeping, we would have a chat. The weather was cold and brisk and so we didn't get out as much as I would have liked. I told Natalie that Penny was having everyone over to her house for some lunch after the christening on Sunday. 'There will probably be about fourteen people there,' I said.
'Well, if I can be of any help preparing the food, let me know!' Natalie replied kindly.
'Charlie and I are going in Madison's car, along with Penny. So if you would like to come with us, you can, Natalie!' I said.
My friends from work would be there along with some other friends and family, and so the cottage

would be a bit crowded. Penny therefore offered to have it in her house, which I thanked her for.

Sunday came around very quickly, and as I was sitting in the church, it was very difficult to hold back the tears that I felt, heavy in my eyes. Carter would have been a proud man to be sitting here alongside me. I quickly composed myself as my friends and I walked towards the Alter. Charlie didn't make a sound as he was being christened. When the organ music played, his little eyes would glare all around the church with amazement. As we were leaving the church, Madison took Charlie in his arms, and I heard a lady's voice saying, 'You must be a very proud father to have such a lovely, content little baby.' Madison just laughed, brushing off the comment.
We all arrived at Penny's house, and she had made such a beautiful spread of food for everyone. To my surprise, there was a big cake sitting in the corner of the room on a table. The cake was in the shape of a teddy bear. Once again I felt the tears spring to my eyes. I was so lucky to have such amazing, caring people in my life.
'I am glad you like it!' Zara said, as she came up behind me and squeezed my hand, obviously having noticed the slight tear roll down my cheek. 'I just wanted to do something special for the baby!'

Before I knew it, springtime had arrived, and every day after lunch I would put Charlie into his pram, and off we would go for long walks in the countryside and down into the valley. I felt like myself again. I had finally come to terms with the fact that Carter was gone, and I needed to start thinking about Charlie and myself, and set our plans for the future. Penny called into the cottage every evening after work. She had Charlie spoilt – always buying him some little toy or something to wear every week, without fail. I tried so many times to tell her to stop, but there was just no talking to her. She loved Charlie so much, and the feeling was mutual. Natalie would also call most evenings, and I would enjoy a coffee with her. She loved being around Charlie as well. His little eyes would light up as Natalie walked through the door. After he had his bath at night, just before he went to sleep, Natalie would cradle and sing to him. Charlie loved being in the company of other people. It was a change of scenery from me. He loved the attention! Natalie suggested going down to the waterfall in the valley on Sunday with a picnic, and even though Charlie didn't understand, he still smiled, like the happy little boy he always was. 'Would you mind if we invited Penny and Madison?' I asked Natalie. To which she replied, 'Yes, Anna. Good idea. That would be lovely.'

The following morning, I went into the city and as I promised, took Charlie into my office to see everyone. Zara, as always, was so excited to see Charlie. 'It's lovely to see you Anna. Charlie just gets bigger and bigger every time I see him. He is just the image of Carter,' she said.
'Yes, he is very much so,' I replied, remembering that I had come to terms with everything, and I had to hold myself together. Just as Zara was about to say something, I heard a voice from behind me – 'Well, well, how is my god-son doing?' And just then, Madison appeared in front of me, with that big smile. 'I was just thinking about you!' I said, as Madison lifted Charlie out of his carry seat. 'How would you

like to join us next Sunday? Natalie and I are going to the waterfall with Charlie for a picnic, and Penny is possibly going to come along too?'
'Count me in!' Madison giggled.

I didn't stay very long in the office, as I wanted to call in and see Rose. I got home around 5pm, and noticed Penny's car was parked outside her house. Penny normally got home around 6pm. So I wondered why she was home so early.
'Hi, Anna,' Penny said, as Charlie and I walked up her path. 'There's no need to be worried. I just wanted to surprise you by making dinner for you coming home tonight.'
With relief pulsing through my body, I responded, 'Oh, Penny, you really didn't have to. I thought there was something wrong.'
'Anna, you always cook for me, and I thought you could come and enjoy a treat at my house. So come in and sit down. Dinner will be ready soon, and I also have some baby dinners for Charlie.' So I had dinner at Penny's house. She had made a lasagne and salad. I asked her about going for the picnic with Natalie and Madison on Sunday. She loved the idea. 'I'll be there!' she said.
After a lovely meal at Penny's, Charlie and I headed home. I had a set routine for Charlie every night and he normally went to bed about 7.30pm. As I arrived home, Madison's car was parked outside the cottage.
'Hi Anna! I hope you don't mind me calling,' he said.
'Not at all. In fact, I am glad you did. Come in and keep an eye on Charlie while I run his bath.' Madison and I were standing in the living room and he said, 'I wanted to have a chat with you today, Anna, but let's get Charlie settled first.' Madison then asked when I would be coming back to work. 'I really need

to talk to Joe about that,' I said. 'I hope he can extend my leave until January. I am going to call in again next week to ask him.'

After we got Charlie bathed and into bed, the two of us sat talking.
'I'm going to Donegal next week to look at a house, and I was going to ask if you wanted to come, Anna. I have been thinking about buying something down South for a long time, and I feel now is the right time.'
'Yes, I will come. Though I don't really want to bring Charlie, because it is such a long distance. But I'm sure Penny would look after him while I am away,' I said.
'Thank you, Anna. I really appreciate it,' Madison said, with his favourite grin.

I lay awake thinking to myself most of that night. I was wondering why Madison had asked *me* to come to Donegal with him. I didn't want to say anything to Penny until we had gotten Sunday over us. I was so unsure about how she was going to react. However, after all, Madison and I are just really good friends, *right?* Although, in part of my mind, I knew Penny liked him.

Natalie arrived at my cottage shortly after 1.30pm on Sunday afternoon. Penny then followed. Madison was just running a bit late. I couldn't stop thinking about how I was going to tell Penny about my visit to Donegal with Madison, but the sooner I told her, the better. It was a beautiful day. The sun was shining, and my mind drifted back to when Carter and I spent our last day together, just here, at the waterfall. 'Come on, Anna!' Penny said, as I stopped

to gaze around the beautiful scenery. Madison was leading the way and was carrying Charlie in his baby seat. Natalie asked if I was all right, clearly noticing my everlasting gaze around the waterfall.
When we had stopped walking, Penny got the food out of the basket and set it on the picnic table. Everything looked so perfect, and Natalie and I took some photographs. I watched as both of my friends played with Charlie. 'They do make a lovely couple, don't they?' I half whispered to Natalie. Just at that moment, Madison laughed and said to Penny, 'You will definitely be kept busy next Saturday with this little chap!'
'Oh no....' I thought to myself. I hadn't told her yet. Everyone went silent after seeing Penny's confused look. 'Am I missing something?' Penny asked, clearly confused. Madison shot looks my way, as if to say, *'You haven't asked her yet...have you?'*
As I cleared my throat, I then responded, 'I am so sorry. I was going to have a chat with you later tonight to ask you could you possibly look after Charlie next Saturday?' Penny, still confused as to why this was a problem and probably how Madison knew before she did, looked at Madison as he said, 'Look, I must apologise. Please let me explain.' Madison then explained to Penny that he had asked me to go to Donegal next Saturday to view some property. I could see that Penny felt somewhat hurt after Madison had finished, but she still politely replied, 'Yes, of course. It would be my pleasure to take care of Charlie for the day!'
We enjoyed the rest of the day, but Penny seemed distant. She excused herself when we all arrived back at the cottage. 'Can we talk, Anna?' Madison said, after Penny had left. 'I am so sorry for saying to Penny about Donegal. I honestly thought you had

already mentioned it to her.' I could feel anger in my blood, something I had never felt before with Madison. 'Look, can you please just leave it, Madison. Oh and also, would you mind if I didn't go with you next week?' I didn't mean to be angry with Madison. In actual fact it was myself I was angry at. How could I be so stupid? I knew how much Penny liked Madison, and I went and stabbed her in the back. However I couldn't help being angry. I then went on to explain to Madison how much Penny liked him, and that I couldn't upset her. I didn't know whether I should tell him this or not. However as always, I was doing it anyway. Madison shook his head and said, 'Anna, I am sorry, but you see, I am...fond of you.'

If I thought there was anger racing through my blood five minutes ago, it was now pulsing through my veins, numbing my entire frame, as I cried, 'NO! Stop it now. I can't believe I am hearing this. Please go Madison. I don't want to talk about this anymore.'

As I got into bed after Madison left, I felt sick to my stomach. I didn't know what I was going to do about this. How was I going to sort this out? When I thought about it, I knew in my heart all along that Madison wanted more than just a friendship with me.

The following evening when Penny called in to see me, I explained everything to her. Penny listened for a while without saying anything, which made me slightly nervous. Then finally, after me doing all the talking, Penny sighed and said, 'Somehow I guessed that Madison was getting closer with you and growing very fond of you. Please don't feel you have to explain yourself or explain on Madison's behalf.'

After that, we didn't talk about it anymore. However, I did phone Madison the next evening and we had a very long chat about how he was sorry and that he was worried we wouldn't still be friends after this. It was safe to say we both wanted to put all of this behind us.

The next week came, and Madison went off to Donegal by himself to view the house as he had planned. I just couldn't bring myself to go with him. I knew he was upset that I didn't go, but it was for the best. Before he left, I told him to drive safe, take some pictures and to call me when he got back. Penny and I went into the city to do some shopping and have lunch whilst Charlie spent the day with Natalie. This was really the first time I had properly left Charlie with Natalie, but I had to get used to doing this before I went back to work. As I dropped Charlie off, Natalie said, 'Now go and enjoy your day, Anna. Charlie will be fine.' I knew he would be fine. Natalie was amazing with Charlie, and he loved her a lot. Although I still worried, as mothers do. 'But...' I said, and was interrupted by Natalie, 'But nothing. Remember when you go back to work he will be with me every day. So go!'

As Penny and I were walking around the shops, she said, 'I take it Madison went to Donegal this morning then?'
'Yes, he did,' I replied. 'He is going to call me when he gets back.' I knew I shouldn't bring this whole situation back up again, but I just couldn't stop myself. 'Look, Penny, Madison and I are best friends,' I said. 'He was Carter's best friend, and has been there for me just like you have. I do hope that in time, he will find a nice girl.' To which Penny bluntly replied, 'Yes, me too, Anna.'

The subject was quickly changed, and Penny asked if I would like to go to the cinema on Friday. 'Yes, that would be nice, and then maybe we could go for a glass of wine after?' We finished looking around the shops and then went for lunch.
'Why do you keep looking at your watch Anna?' Penny asked.
I hadn't even noticed that I was checking my watch every couple of minutes. 'I just don't want to be away from Charlie for too long,' I explained. Penny laughed slightly and then gave a sigh. 'Please, Anna, you must try to relax. You know how much Natalie loves Charlie, and you need time out as well. To be honest, I bet he is having a great time. He loves all the attention!' I must say that I did enjoy my day out with Penny.

We got home around 4.30pm and I phoned Natalie to say I was home. 'Charlie is just having his tea. Then I will bring him round at about 5pm or so,' she said.

Natalie arrived at my house shortly after 5pm. 'How was your day?' she asked. 'We had a lovely day,' I said. 'Although, I must admit, I did miss my little boy!'
'You should start going out more often, 'Natalie said. 'You know I will always take care of the little man.'
I noticed Charlie's little cheeks were glowing and he wouldn't let go of his teething ring. Even though his mouth was sore, he didn't cry much.

The following morning, as I was feeding Charlie breakfast, I noticed two tiny white teeth that had just broken through his gum at the lower part of his mouth.

'Oh Charlie!' I squealed excitedly. 'You have got two teeth!' I am sure the child thought I was raving bonkers. I couldn't wait to tell Penny. Just as I was about to take Charlie for a walk over to Penny's, as she was off work, the phone rang. It was Joe.
'I am so glad you called,' I said. 'I know I am meant to be going back to work in November, but I wanted to ask could my leave be extended until the beginning of February?'
Joe knew I wanted to extend my leave. However, I don't think he realised by how long, as he sounded shocked, saying, 'Yes, Anna, that shouldn't be a problem. Just make sure you come back to us!' he laughed.
I felt that I needed to be with Charlie that bit longer. I wasn't ready to leave him with Natalie every day yet. 'I was going to call into the office during the week to have a chat with you,' I said. 'But there is no need now that you have called.'
I went on to tell Joe about how well Charlie was getting on, and I obviously had to tell him about his first two teeth!
'Why don't you call in later and see us?' I said.
'Yeah, I would like that Anna. I will pop over to see you both later this afternoon,' Joe replied.

Charlie was getting restless, as he was ready in his pram to go over and see Penny. He started getting anxious while I was on the phone. So I hung up and then we both went over to Penny's, where we spent a few hours.
I told Penny about Charlie's teeth and how I had got my leave from work extended. 'Penny lifted Charlie out of his push chair saying, 'Wow, you're getting big Charlie!' She then asked was everything still okay for the cinema on Friday. We discussed how we

needed to book a taxi to take us home, since we would be going for a couple of glasses of wine after the cinema. Then Charlie and I headed home. I was just in the door as Joe arrived. 'My goodness,' he said. 'Charlie sure is getting big and by the looks of things, he will be up walking in no time at all!'
We were sitting talking about work and what was going on in the office, and then Joe mentioned Madison. He asked had I heard from him. To which I replied, 'Yes, he was going down to Donegal yesterday to look at some property, and I haven't heard from him since. He said he was going to ring me when he got home.'
'Yes,' Joe said. 'I always thought he was going to move down to Donegal.' A little shocked, I said, 'No, I think it's just a holiday home. Well, I assume it is.'
'You will be going to the Christmas dinner, Anna, won't you?' Joe asked.
'Yes of course. I wouldn't miss it!' I laughed. Joe then went on his way, telling me to call into the office to talk to Zara, who would be arranging Christmas dinner, no doubt. 'You know what she's like,' Joe said. 'Everything has to be done early and according to plan.' 'Yes. No problem. Thanks Joe. See you soon!' I waved goodbye.
It was Tuesday before I heard from Madison. He called to tell me about the house he had gone to see in Donegal. 'It is beautiful, Anna, and not too far away from the beach. Maybe you and Charlie could go down and see it sometime!'
'Yeah sure,' I said. 'That would be nice.' Madison then explained that he had bought the house and that he would have to go back down during the week to sign the papers for it. It was an elderly couple he had bought it from. 'I would like to refurbish it, but

that can wait until next spring and then I will make a start.'

Once again, it was time for the Christmas dinner with the guys from work. Penny and Zara both laughed as they pulled the crackers at our table.
'Why don't you join in, Anna?' Zara said.
'It looks like Anna has pulled her own cracker!' said Penny.
I couldn't help but notice the handsome guy who was seated at the table opposite us. He had short dark hair with silver strands through it. As both my friends giggled quite loudly, the guy looked over at us and said, 'You girls seem to be having fun.' Penny, obviously having found her inner self-confidence with the multiple glasses of wine she had had throughout the night, said, 'Why don't you and your friends come over and join us? We can have fun together.' I could feel my cheeks burning with embarrassment, and I wasn't quite sure why.
Once our meal was over, a few of the guys came over to join us. Once everyone had been introduced, and Penny had arranged the seating, I found she had *coincidently* placed me beside the guy I had been glancing at throughout the night. I had found out his name was Ben. As everyone began chatting to one another, I noticed Madison was leaving the table with Joe. They made their way to the bar, where they ended up staying for the rest of the night.
'Why are you leaving us, Madison?' Maria asked. Maria was the replacement, who was covering my leave at the office. She was a lovely young blonde lady, who was a lot of fun. Madison didn't answer her. 'Has this got anything to do with me?' I subtly whispered to Penny.

'Look. Stop worrying about it, Anna. Just enjoy yourself.' A short time later, Ben asked me would I like to go out to the lobby bar where it was a bit quieter. I excused myself from the table and joined him. As we sat, having a glass of wine, Ben began to tell me that he had come back to Belfast six months ago, after working as a medic in London. 'I am sure that was very interesting!' I said.
'Yes, it was indeed. But to be honest, I am glad to be home again.' Ben told me a lot about himself as we were sitting there. He had been dating a girl for over two years. Although it turned out they both wanted something different, and so they decided to call it off. This played a part in Ben returning to Belfast, and he was currently staying in his parents' house until he gets his own place.
'Tell me, Anna, what do you do in your spare time?' Ben said, as he leaned in close.
'Well, I spend a lot of my time with my little boy, Charlie,' I said, not knowing, and for some reason slightly apprehensive of, what his reaction would be.
'You have a son?' Ben asked.
'Yes, I do. He will be one, come the end of January.' I replied. Then I paused as I saw Ben staring into my eyes, willing me to tell more about Charlie. I told Ben a lot about Charlie and how Carter died in a road accident. Ben exclaimed his apologies about Carter, and I then went on to talk about Penny and how we had grown up together. Ben had obviously noticed how Madison had swiftly left the table earlier on in the evening, as he said, 'Your friend Madison didn't stay too long once my friends and I joined your table earlier on.'
'Please don't take that personally,' I half laughed. 'You see, I first met Carter through Madison. They were work colleagues and good friends.' I didn't

want to talk past tense anymore, so I quickly changed the subject.

'I am going back to work after Charlie's first birthday,' I said. 'My boss, Joe, who was at the table earlier with Madison, has been more than kind to me, and I do enjoy my work and we all get on really well at the office.'

'Who will take care of Charlie when you go back to work?' Ben asked.

'A good friend of mine,' I replied. 'Her name is Natalie. She has her own nursery, and so she will be taking him there every day. Charlie loves her, which is the main thing and it'll be good for Charlie to be with other children too.'

'So, more about you,' I said. 'Do you have any brothers or sisters?'

'I have one sister,' Ben replied. 'Her name is Eva, and her husband is called Phil. They have two twin girls who are five – Lucy and Ellie,' he smiled.

'What lovely names,' I said.

'Yes, they are lovely girls. I am spending Christmas at Eva's house this year. I am looking forward to it. Phil is a really nice guy, and he is so good to Eva, and an excellent dad. He too works as a medic. However, he is based in a different hospital than me. Eva is a full time mum at home. She loves spending time with the girls,' Ben said.

As the evening was coming to an end, Ben asked me would I like to meet up again to go for lunch sometime. I told him that I would like that very much. We exchanged numbers so that we could keep in touch.

'Anna!' I heard Penny call, as she stumbled round the corner, quite clearly having had a good night!

'We must be going now,' she said, words slurred. 'Our taxi is outside.'
'Thank you for a lovely evening, Ben,' I said, as I gave him a quick hug goodbye.
Ben told me that he hoped we could meet up for that lunch date soon, and that he also had a good night. Penny was staying at mine that night and I knew I was about to get asked a thousand questions about Ben. Natalie was reading when we got home. As we walked through the door, she asked how our night was.
'Anna had an *amazing* time,' Penny giggled. 'She spent her night with a handsome guy out in the lobby...just the two of them.' Then she flopped onto the sofa.
'Oh Penny, leave it until the morning!' I said, rolling my eyes.
Natalie then went on to tell me that Charlie had been very good all night, as always. 'I didn't put him to bed until after 9pm. He was having too much fun to sleep, playing with his building blocks.'
Penny lifted her head off the sofa and said, yawning, 'I'm going to go to sleep now.' I laughed, and asked Natalie would she like to stay too. I could make the sofa bed up for her. Before I went to get ready for bed, I went into Charlie's room to check on him. I gave him a kiss on the head. He looked so peaceful. I quietly slipped out of the room, and as I was walking to the bathroom I looked into my room to find Penny had passed out on top of my bed. Once I had brushed my teeth and washed, I tried to wake Penny to move her, and she responded, mumbling, 'Oh Anna, I am just too comfy here. Please just leave me be.' I could hear Natalie laughing as I tried to move my friend to make room for me. She was lying

diagonally across my bed. It was impossible for me to squeeze in.
It was safe to say that I didn't get much sleep that night. I lay awake, listening to Penny snoring, and mostly thinking about Ben. Somehow I felt guilty that I had agreed to meet him again. But I kept telling myself Carter had gone and that I couldn't keep living in the past.

The next morning, I heard a little voice calling, 'Mama, Mama!'
I went down the hall to Charlie's room and brought him into the kitchen to make breakfast. I put him into his highchair, and as I looked at my little boy, I could see he was getting more and more like Carter every day. 'Are you alright, Anna?' Natalie said, as she walked round the corner, to join us in the kitchen. 'You seem so...so lost in thought.'
'No I am fine, Natalie. I take it Penny is still asleep?' I replied, taking my eyes off Charlie. Just at that moment, a happy Penny wandered into the kitchen saying, 'Good morning ladies!'
There was a massive smile on her face, which, to be honest, I was not expecting considering the consumption of alcohol on her part the previous night.
'Someone seems in a good mood,' Natalie said, also clearly noticing Penny's grin.
'I must say, Anna, I had such a lovely sleep. I probably kept you up. I am really sorry if I did,' Penny said with a laugh.
'Oh, I tried, but you were having none of it!' I replied, also laughing.
Natalie was making breakfast while I was feeding Charlie. Penny was nursing her sore head and making herself some coffee.

'Don't you want anything to eat?' I asked.
'No, I couldn't eat anything at the moment. I can't wait to hear about last night with Ben!' Penny replied.
'Who's Ben?' Natalie asked.
Both Penny and Natalie seemed excited as I began telling them about Ben.
'He sounds like a prince charming!' Natalie said.
'Plus he is good looking!' Penny added, laughing.
They asked when I would be seeing my new friend again, and Penny then brought up the subject of Madison. 'Why did Madison leave the table last night?'
'Honestly, Penny, I have no idea. Although somehow it feels like my fault...like it always is.' I sighed.
'Maybe he just doesn't want you rushing into anything with Ben,' Penny said.
This somewhat annoyed me. We had only just met and I think it is time for me to move on and continue living my life. It wasn't fair for Madison to get involved and get annoyed over something that is none of his business. Madison had always said, *'one day Anna, you will have to start going out because Carter wouldn't want you living your life alone like this.'*
'I am really happy for you, Anna. It's about time you started living your life again, and plus, you will always have Natalie and I to rely on when you want to go out,' Penny said, grinning from ear to ear. Honestly, you would think Penny had found herself a man. She was so happy. At the moment, Ben and I were just friends. But time will tell.
The conversation then moved onto Maria, from last night. 'Maria is a lovely girl, isn't she Anna?' Penny said. 'Yes, she is. She got along so well with everyone. I am just hoping she doesn't steal my job permanently!' I laughed.

Penny and Natalie spent most of that day at the cottage, playing with Charlie and chatting. I couldn't believe Christmas was just three days away. I was so excited to spend it with my son.

Later that night, after Natalie had left, I got a phone call, and who was it? Ben. I couldn't believe it.
'Hello, Anna,' he said. 'If you aren't busy tomorrow, would you like to meet up for lunch?' Penny, who was now standing beside me, listening intently into our phone call, was doing that grin again. The excitement on her face was unreal.
'That would be lovely,' I replied. I could feel the butterflies in my tummy.
After I got off the phone, Penny nearly exploded.
'ANNA!' she squealed. 'I am so glad you said yes to him. It didn't take long for him to get back in contact with you. Someone is keen!'
'Penny, I need to ask you a question,' I started. 'Do you honestly think it is too soon for me to start seeing someone again?'
'Look, Anna,' Penny slightly shouted with her best *'angry'* face on. 'You need to stop this. You can't just sit here and live in the past. Please, let's not go through this again. You better go with Ben tomorrow, and do not spend the time looking at your watch, worrying about Charlie or worrying about anything else for that matter. Charlie will be fine with me. It is just lunch you are going for. It's nothing serious. Ben just wants to get to know you better.' Penny, slightly flustered, but quite clearly feeling proud of her little rant, sat back and took a deep draw of air.

The next day, when I arrived at the restaurant, Ben was already there, looking handsome as ever. 'It's lovely to see you again, Anna. I am so glad you could come today!' Ben said, as he got out of his seat to give me a quick hug and peck on the cheek. As I sat down at the table opposite him, I said, 'How have you been?'

'I am fine, and you?' he said, smiling.

'I've been fine. I have been doing my Christmas shopping, getting last minute things for friends and Penny, and taking Charlie to see Santa.'

'I bet he liked that!' Ben laughed.

'Yeah, he was bouncing with excitement,' I replied. 'Though he doesn't understand just yet what it's all about. But he did love it.'

Ben and I spent the afternoon together, talking about our lives, our likes and dislikes, and to my amazement, we actually had a lot in common. Just then I noticed the clock in the corner of the room. It was 5pm! Well at least I listened to Penny and didn't keep looking at my watch. However I really had to be going home now. I explained to Ben that I had to go home and get Charlie his tea and let Penny go home.

'I am sure we could meet up again, Anna, once Christmas is over!' Ben said.

I smiled and once again said yes to his offer as he walked me to my car and placed a kiss upon my cheek. 'Have a wonderful Christmas, and thanks again for coming today. I will see you soon, okay?' He said as he walked towards his car.

I arrived home to find Penny had already made Charlie his tea. I apologised for being late and started going on about how I would have been home earlier but I was having such a lovely day and I didn't realise the time.

'Don't you worry yourself, Anna,' Penny said. 'Charlie and I had a great afternoon. Madison called and we took him for a walk, and before you say anything, we made sure he was wrapped up well in his winter suit! I am so glad you had a good day, Anna. This is just what you needed.'
'What did Madison say?' I asked penny. 'I didn't know he was calling today.'
'He just popped in to make sure everything was alright for Christmas day, and to see if you needed anything,' Penny said.
'Did you tell him I was out for lunch with Ben?' I asked, finding it hard to mask the worry in my voice. I wasn't even sure why I was worried about him, knowing this. I just couldn't help it. *'We have been over this...'* I told myself.
'Yes, Anna I did. Anyway, he saw you and Ben sitting together at the Christmas dinner. You know he was watching you both all of that evening!' Penny said.
'I will phone him later and have a chat with him, once I get Charlie off to bed,' I said.

Later that night, I rang Madison. He seemed so distant on the phone, like he didn't really care what I was saying. 'Is everything alright?' I asked.
'Of course it is. Why do you ask that?' Madison replied, uninterested.
'You just don't sound like yourself.' Madison was so quiet and so, as I continued, I had to be blunt. 'Is this something to do with Ben?' I asked.
'Look Anna,' Madison started. 'I can't tell you what to do with your life, but...'
'But nothing,' I interrupted. 'You always said it was time for me to start moving on. So why aren't you happy for me?' I was now sobbing uncontrollably.

‘I am so sorry, Anna. Please forgive me. I just don’t want to lose you and Charlie,’ Madison said, apologetically.
‘Madison, you and I have been friends for a long time now,’ I said. ‘I want our friendship to last a lifetime. Besides, you’re Charlie’s godfather. So he is never getting away from you!’ I laughed through the tears. ‘So can we please put this silly argument behind us now? I miss my best friend and I am tired of this.’ We ended our phone call on a much brighter note, and I laughed and cried at the same time as I hung up.

Christmas morning finally came. Charlie awakened early, and as I went into his room I could see his smiley face popping out from under the blanket. I brought him into the living room to see all the presents that were left for him. Penny had been up and lit the Christmas tree. It was perfect. ‘Come on, let’s open the presents!’ Penny squealed excitedly, taking Charlie’s hand. Madison had bought Charlie a beautiful rocking horse. I watched as Penny held him on the horse as he rocked back and forth. The giggles of them both were wonderful.
‘Let’s open the other gifts too!’ I said to Charlie. But he would not let go of this rocking horse. He had no interest in anything else. He was just happy rocking to and fro.
As promised, Madison arrived early to have breakfast with us. As he handed me my gift, he placed a kiss upon my brow. ‘Merry Christmas, Anna,’ he said, as he walked towards Penny and Charlie. I opened my present to find it was a stunning gold chain and locket. I carefully opened the locket. Inside was a photograph of Madison,

Charlie and Penny. 'This is so beautiful,' I gasped as I looked at Madison. 'When was this picture taken?'
'Oh, Anna, that was the day you went out with Ben,' Penny said. 'Remember I told you Madison and I took Charlie for a walk? Well we went and got the picture taken that day.'
'I love it. It is so special,' I said. 'Come and help me put it on, Penny.' As we exchanged gifts, Penny threw her arms around Madison as he was sitting on the floor beside her and Charlie.
'Thank you so much,' she said. 'Look, Anna. Look what Madison got me!' It was two tickets to go and see a concert in Dublin. 'You have to come with me, Anna!' Penny was screaming and dancing around.
After breakfast was over, we all headed over to Penny's. We took along some toys to keep Charlie entertained. Little did we know, but the real excitement was about to begin. We had no sooner got to Penny's, than Charlie began to take his first steps. Madison was struggling with toys under his arm and holding Charlie's hand. Then I heard the crash of the toys hitting the floor as Madison waddled along behind Charlie, who was pottering from the middle of Penny's living room to the sofa. Charlie then broke free from Madison's supportive hands, and started walking towards me, giggling away to himself.
'Mama!' He called, with his little arms outstretched. We all went silent as he fell into my arms. I could feel his heart racing as he clung to me.
'That was amazing Charlie,' I said. 'You are just amazing.' The tears were now rolling down my face. After that, there was no stopping my little boy that day. Now that he was walking, he just spent hours pottering around, getting used to these newfound feet and showing off. Everything was amazing. The

dinner was beautiful. Penny had the table set in such a sophisticated display and she had even got our names on placemats! Later that evening, Maria arrived at Penny's. It was lovely to see her again. Natalie called also, bringing Charlie even more presents. Natalie couldn't believe her eyes when she saw Charlie up walking. Her hands were certainly going to be full, having to look after this little boy. Just on that note, Maria then said, 'It won't be long until you're back to work, Anna. I'm sure going to miss working at the office. I have had a really good time and met loads of wonderful people.'
'Yes, it won't be long,' I replied. 'But I will only be back three days a week. So I am sure Joe would be happy to have you stay on.'
'I would like that. However, I think I would need something more permanent, Anna,' she said.
Penny and Maria had been planning their New Year's Eve night out for a few weeks now. Madison had decided to go out with them, along with Maria's partner, Shane.
'Would you not change your mind and come with us, Anna?' Penny and Maria pleaded. The two of them loved a good night out.
'To be honest, I think I would rather just stay in with Charlie,' I said. 'Besides, I have Natalie to keep me company that evening.'

After Christmas was all over, it was nice to relax and spend New Year's Eve with Charlie and Natalie. Shortly after midnight, my phone rang. It was Ben.
'Happy New Year, Anna!' he said.
'Thank you,' I replied laughing. 'And a very happy one to you too.' We chatted for over an hour, as Natalie entertained Charlie. Ben told me he would phone me again during the week to organise a catch

up. When I got off the phone, Natalie commented, 'Penny didn't phone to wish us a happy new year!' she laughed.
'Penny is probably too busy having a good time, singing and more than likely dancing! No doubt we will hear all tomorrow,' I replied.

The time had passed so quickly since that night. I was now starting work tomorrow and Charlie had settled into nursery with Natalie. It was so strange seeing all my colleagues on a regular basis again. It was going to take some time to get used to this routine. The bond between us, and the jokes within the office, hadn't changed at all since I left. And it was no surprise to anyone in the office that Ben was the new man in my life. Even Madison seemed to be happy for me, as everyone was asking questions about this new guy. Although Madison was happy for me, he explained that he was still standing by the fact he didn't want me to rush into anything too fast.

I felt quite nervous the first time Ben introduced me to his parents. They were called James and Peggy. However, I must say they were truly lovely people. They made Charlie and I feel very at home and more than welcome in their house. On the same day, I got to meet Ben's sister, Eva, and her husband Phil, and the twins. In no time at all, Charlie had made friends with the twins, Lucy and Ellie.
So many things had changed since I left the office to go on maternity. For one, Zara and Connor had moved to Newcastle where they got married and now have a home. Madison is now dating Paula, who is a school Teacher. They are pretty loved up as far as I am aware, which I am thrilled about.

Penny and I sat talking about how much has changed over the two years, so nostalgically, in my cottage a few weeks after meeting Ben's parents.
'Where does the time go?' Penny asked.
'Time is just passing so quickly,' I replied. 'And what about you, Penny? You haven't found anyone yet!'
Penny gave a smile and rolled her eyes.
'Now, Anna,' she said, 'I do quite like the new dental surgeon...Johnny!'
'Penny!' I squealed. 'Come on. Tell me more. Why haven't you mentioned this before?'
'Well, I wanted to make sure he was interested in me first!' Penny replied, seemingly embarrassed.
'And is he?' I asked.
'Yes, he is. I have had a few lunch dates with him,' Penny said.
'My goodness, Penny, you kept that quiet.' I was now sitting on the edge of my seat, thinking, I can't wait to meet him!
'Now, steady on, Anna!' Penny laughed. 'It has only been a few weeks!'
Penny and I talked into the early hours, once again about what the future holds.

Monday came around again, and I was now heading to the office after dropping Charlie off at Natalie's. I worked hard through most of the morning and headed to the staff room for lunch at 12.30pm. I got a shock that I was not expecting that day in the staff room - Madison had informed me that he and Paula were thinking about moving down to Donegal.
'Wow! That's a massive surprise...' I said to Madison, trying to hide my discomfort. 'But what about your job and Paula's class?' I said, not knowing what to say.

'Nothing has been set in stone yet, Anna. But we have been talking about it a lot and I wanted you to be the first to know,' Madison said.
I felt hurt at the thought of losing one of my closest friends, not to mention the closest friend that Carter had also. I knew I would miss him so much. My mind kept drifting back to the day I first met Carter. Madison had been the one to introduce that amazing man into my life. I was now getting emotional as I tried to fight back the tears I could feel brewing in my eyes. I found myself lying awake most of that night, thinking to myself '*is it my fault Madison is moving away?*'

The next day, Ben came to the cottage. Charlie was sleeping and so we got a chance to sit down and have a proper chat. I told Ben about how I felt about the Madison situation. I explained that Madison is going to make a new life for him and Paula, just like I hope to do with him.
'Anna. I'm sorry to be so abrupt, but let's talk about the future,' Ben interrupted, unexpectedly.
I walked towards him and put my arms around his neck, looking into his eyes, slightly worried, and nervous about what was to follow. 'What is it, Ben?' I asked.
'Anna, I am asking you to be my wife,' he said.
My heart stopped.
'I wanted to propose in a more romantic way, but I can't wait any longer,' Ben said.
I said yes, straight away. I didn't even have to think about it.
'We should keep this to ourselves until after Charlie's birthday party,' Ben said.
We had already planned Charlie's fourth birthday party for next week. It was going to be at Natalie's

nursery and I had invited all of his little friends. It was going to be difficult keeping our secret from Penny, but I had to hold it until the day of Charlie's party. Penny had called earlier that morning to take Charlie to get his birthday present, and my, this little boy sure knew what he wanted! Penny was not aware that Charlie would want a rabbit, when she took him shopping for his birthday, but of course she could never say no to his little face! 'Anna, I hope you don't mind,' Penny had said when she brought him home from their day of shopping, 'but Charlie said he wanted the rabbit for his birthday and I couldn't disappoint him!'

The following morning as I was in the kitchen making Charlie his breakfast, I heard him call 'Mummy, Mummy! Come here.'
I ran outside to see what was wrong, to find my son standing, trembling.
'Are you alright, Charlie?' I exclaimed.
'Yes Mummy! Come and look in Queenie's hutch. She has had little babies,' said Charlie.
It was overwhelming watching the excitement on my son's face as he counted the tiny, newborn rabbits. I had to fight back the tears as Charlie and I counted how many little ones Queenie had. 'I can see four, Charlie,' I said.
'No Mummy, there are five!' Charlie shouted, excitedly.
I counted them again and could still only see four.
'But Mummy, there are five – Daddy said five! Can't you see my Daddy? He is standing beside you,' Charlie asked.
Pulses began racing up and down my spine.
'Charlie, why did you say that?' I asked.

'I always see my Daddy,' Charlie began. 'He comes to watch me play when I am alone.'

I had never told Charlie about how his father died. I only told him that his Daddy was in heaven. I wanted to wait until he was old enough to understand. I had been sorting through photographs one evening and I had showed Charlie photos of his father.
With all these thoughts rolling about my head, I had to compose myself. I couldn't let Charlie see me upset, and again I had to remind myself not to live in the past. I had to think about my future with Ben.
'Would you like to ring Penny and tell her about your new baby rabbits?' I asked Charlie.
'Oh yes, Mummy. Please let me talk to Penny!' Charlie squealed happily.
As I picked up the receiver and dialled Penny's number, I watched Charlie, as his little hands began to shake, excited to tell the good news about these little rabbits. The excitement on his face was unbelievable.
'Penny, Penny! Come and see the babies', he shouted. 'Queenie has had her babies. Come now! Penny, please!'
I could hear Penny laughing on the line, saying, 'I will be at the cottage in ten minutes, Charlie.'
I couldn't wait to tell her what my son had said about Carter.
Charlie was now leading Penny by the hand up to Queenie's hutch. I stood and watched as they counted the rabbits again.
'Yes, Anna, there sure are five,' Penny laughed.
'See, didn't I tell you Mummy!' Charlie chorused, without taking his eyes off the new rabbits.

‘I need to talk to you, Penny,’ I said, no longer laughing.
‘Is everything alright, Anna?’ Penny asked, clearly worried.
‘I’ll go make us a coffee and we can have a chat while Charlie is feeding Queenie,’ I said, as I rushed off to the kitchen.

Penny and I were now sitting at the table in the kitchen, looking out the window at Charlie, happily feeding the rabbits. ‘Today, when Charlie was showing me the rabbits, he said he could see Carter… standing beside me. I was so stunned that these words were coming from my little boy. Then he went on to tell me that his daddy said there were five babies and oh… Penny,’ I sighed, ‘Charlie never even knew his Dad.’
‘Anna, I really don’t know why he would say that. When Natalie comes to pick him up on Monday why don’t you ask her has Charlie ever said anything about Carter?’ Penny said.

As everyone arrived to the nursery that Friday to attend Charlie’s fourth birthday party, my nerves were getting the better of me. In just a few hours, Ben and I were going to announce our engagement. Just on that note, I hadn’t seen Ben arrive yet. Madison and Paula kept all the children happy playing games and Natalie was doing some face painting, while Penny and I prepared the food.
‘Why are you looking so worried?’ Penny asked.
‘It’s not like Ben to be late,’ I answered quickly. ‘I hope he is alright.’
‘Don’t worry, Anna. He will be here. He wouldn’t miss this party for the world!’ Penny assured me.

The weather was dreadful outside. The rain was sure not taking its time to come down. I just wanted Ben to hurry up and come. Though I needed to pull myself together. This was my son's fourth birthday party and I needed to stop thinking the worst. As more and more people started to arrive, Natalie's nursery was filling up. People were enjoying themselves, the kids were having a ball, and most importantly, none of the kids were crying yet!
'Hi everyone,' a voice behind me said, as the door swung open. 'Sorry I am late!'
'Ben!' Charlie called as he ran and jumped into Ben's arms and hugged him.
'How is the birthday boy?' Ben asked, with a big smile as he handed Charlie his present.
'Penny got me a rabbit!' Charlie said, with so much glee in his voice. 'She is called Queenie, and she had baby rabbits today! Come and look at all my presents, Ben!'
Lucy and Ellie were so busy playing that they didn't even realise Ben had arrived. 'Are you alright, Anna?' Ben asked. 'You look worried?'
'I'm fine now,' I replied. 'I was just worried about you. You did say the car was playing up and you know how anxious I get. Everything was racing through my mind!'
'That's why I am late. I had to wait at the garage for over an hour. But never mind. I am here now! Now let's go and see the birthday boy,' Ben said.
Penny was watching as Ben joined in with the kids, playing games.
'He sure will make a wonderful father someday,' Penny said.
I could feel my cheeks blushing as I replied, 'He sure will.'

I started walking towards Ben and said to him quietly, 'Please don't mention about our engagement today, Ben. This isn't the right time. It can wait until another time.'

The party was over in what seemed like a flash. Ben came back to the cottage with Charlie and I after we helped Natalie clear up the nursery. My head was pounding and I just wanted an early night. Ben got Charlie settled into bed and I ran myself a bath. I noticed Ben had put some logs on the fire and dimmed the lights. I didn't say anything. I pretended not to notice. As I lay relaxing in the bath, I heard the front door close. I quickly jumped out of the bath and put on my bathrobe, thinking Ben had left. *'Surely he wouldn't leave without saying goodbye?'* I thought to myself. As I walked into the living room, Ben was placing a large bouquet of red roses in a vase, on the coffee table.
'Ben,' I whispered, 'I thought you had left.'
He gave a slight jump and said, 'Sorry, Anna. The front door slammed with the wind.'
I walked towards him, looking at the flowers sitting on the table beside him. I smiled and said, 'They are really beautiful flowers. What's the occasion?' Then I noticed the little card sitting beside the vase. I opened it. Inside, it said, *'Anna, would you please make me the happiest man alive and become my wife?'* I looked at Ben as he stood there, in the middle of the room, holding that little tiny box in his hands. I could see the glimmer of what was inside the box from the other side of the room.
'Yes.' That was the only word that came out. I couldn't manage anymore.
He placed the engagement ring on my finger. It was breathtaking.

‘I really wanted to surprise you,’ he said, ‘and ask you in a more romantic way.’
‘You surprised me enough,’ I laughed. ‘Ben, this is the happiest I have been in a long time.’ My headache soon lifted as we snuggled up on the couch. I kept looking at the beautiful diamond ring on my finger, asking myself *‘is this a dream?’*
We talked about future plans and set a date for our wedding. I couldn't wait to see Charlie's face when I tell him Ben and I are getting married. He loved Ben and I knew he would be bouncing with excitement! I phoned Penny the following morning before she set off for her date with Johnny.
‘Anna,’ she said, ‘I am so happy for you both and I know you and Ben will be so happy together. I will call and see you when I get back later tonight.’
I then phoned Zara and Natalie to tell them both my good news. After I let them know, I considered ringing Madison. I then quickly decided that it would be best to tell him when he came to the office on Monday. I wanted to see his expression. Over the phone wasn't personal enough.

So, Monday morning came again. I was slightly apprehensive thinking about telling Madison about Ben and I, although I knew I couldn’t talk myself out of it. Madison walked through the door a few minutes later. He had no sooner walked towards my desk as I spluttered out the words ‘Ben and I are getting married!’ I couldn't stop the words spilling out of my mouth.
‘Anna,’ he said, like he had been expecting it, ‘I am very happy for both of you. I have got to know Ben very well and he will make a great husband and fantastic stepdad to Charlie.’

I smiled. Then Madison smiled as he continued saying, 'Hopefully sometime in the future, the three of you can move out of the cottage to a bigger house, as a family.'

Ben's sister, Eva had planned an engagement party for us at the hotel where Ben and I first met. We had agreed that Phil would be best man at our wedding, and Eva, matron of honour. Penny and Natalie were to be my two bridesmaids, and of course Charlie the pageboy, and Lucy and Ellie were going to be flower girls. I wanted to give Madison a special part in the wedding, and so he was overjoyed when I asked him to walk me up the aisle!
'It would be an honour, Anna,' he had said when I asked him.
Now that the date was set for the wedding, everyone was getting excited to start preparing. Over the following months, everyone was so busy helping with the wedding arrangements. I was looking forward to the day I would become Ben's wife. *'The day I would finally become a wife...'* I thought to myself, as my mind was fluttering back to when I was looking forward to getting married to Carter.
We had booked our wedding reception at the hotel our engagement party was to be in, and Lorraine, the manager, was just amazing.
'I will take care of everything, Anna,' she said. 'You don't need to worry about a thing. Your day will be perfect!'
Ben and I had talked about moving into the city, but in the back of my mind, I didn't want to leave the country.
'Why don't we extend the cottage Anna. I mean, if you really want to stay here?' Ben had asked.

'Although, we would definitely have to make some major changes.'
'Yes, I agree. After the wedding we can chat to the builders and take it from there,' I said.

Charlie had started primary school and he was settling in pretty well, which was another reason I didn't want to move to the city. Natalie picks Charlie up after school and would look after him until I got home from work every day. I was glad when Ben agreed to stay in the country, even if major changes had to take place in the cottage. I would always regard it as my home. I didn't want to leave.
Time was passing so quickly and Ben had planned a holiday for the three of us. It would be our first family holiday. We had arranged to go down to Donegal to stay in Madison's, over Charlie's school holidays. Ben had arranged with Madison that we would use the house for a week. It was near the beach, which made Charlie want to go even more! Being used to country life, my little boy was totally amazed by the thought of going to the beach.

On the Saturday morning, we arrived in Donegal after a long and tiring car journey, but of course all Charlie wanted to do was go to the beach. As the three of us walked along the beach, Charlie asked, 'Mummy, did Uncle Madison give you and my Daddy his house?'
I looked at Ben and laughed, hinting that maybe he should answer that question. '*Daddy.*' I thought to myself. Why did he say that? Ben started to explain that we only came to Madison's house for a holiday, when suddenly Charlie asked Ben, 'Ben, can I please call you Daddy?'

Charlie had told Ben and I that he had told his school teacher that his mummy was getting married and that he was going to have a Daddy!
'Oh Charlie,' I said. 'Yes, you can call Ben *Daddy*!' I hugged him. The look on Ben's face was priceless. Even though Charlie was young, I had recently explained to him about Carter, his real dad, after the rabbit incident.
The three of us enjoyed our little holiday in Donegal. It was very relaxing...like the calm before the storm, as we were about to go home and have to plan all the last touches of the wedding, which was just around the corner.

We still attended the church in the country, and it was there we were to get married. I had asked Rose to make my wedding dress and also the dresses for the girls. When I had picked them up, they were truly beautiful. I decided to have my flower girls in white and Penny, Eva and Natalie in claret.
Everything was going as planned. Lorraine was making our wedding cake, a beautiful three tier, with the happy couple on top, holding two tiny white doves. Ben and the guys took Charlie to get measured for his little suit.
'He looks so grown up, Anna!' Ben said, after they had come home from the city that day. Penny and Johnny spent many evenings with Ben and I. Penny said we could stay in her house until the cottage was renovated after the wedding. She had arranged to stay at Johnny's place while the cottage was getting revamped, so we wouldn't have to live in what she described as *'an upheaval!'*
'I will definitely take you up on that offer!' I said to Penny, as the four of us were sitting in Penny's house, having coffee.

Once again, it was only weeks before Christmas. I couldn't believe how this year had flew in, and our wedding was now just over a month away! Ben and I took Charlie to see Santa.
Thankfully, with Eva and Penny helping me with the wedding, the preparations were all made. Charlie talked about the wedding more than he talked about Christmas. I was beginning to think he was more excited than me. Ben and I planned to have Christmas in the cottage with Charlie. It was a special time – our first Christmas as a family.
On Christmas Eve, we took presents to Ben's family and our good friends. As this year was coming to a close, the nerves about the wedding were getting the better of me, and not only that, it was going to be Charlie's fifth birthday as well! Penny and I talked about this when we went to see her on Christmas day.
'Well, Anna, that little chap is not bothered about anything other than this wedding. So we will get him something special, and we can give it to him after the wedding service is over,' Penny said.
It was now two days before the wedding.
Ben and I didn't see each other prior to the wedding, but he phoned me on the eve of the big day.
'My goodness,' Ben said. 'You sound like a bundle of nerves, Anna. You're making me nervous!'
'I am sorry Ben,' I half laughed. 'I just want everything to go to plan.'
'Calm down. This time tomorrow you are going to be *Mrs Collins*!' Ben said. 'Now you just get some sleep and make sure Madison has you at the church on time tomorrow!' Ben giggled. My heart skipped a beat. The sound of Ben's voice was always so reassuring. He always said the right things to make me feel so at ease.

The big day had arrived. Eva and the twins were at the cottage before 8am. Natalie and Penny had stayed overnight with me. I looked at the twins sitting on the couch, beside Charlie, dressed in their little wedding outfits.
Of course, Charlie wouldn't stop asking, 'When am I going in the big car, Mummy?'
Lucy and Ellie giggled at Charlie. I was glad they had each other for company today. Eva helped me get ready, and finally placed my veil on my head.
'Please don't cry, Anna. You will ruin your makeup,' she said, seeing the slight tears in my eyes. I was just so overwhelmed.
'I am sorry. I'm not upset. I am just so happy!' I said. I couldn't wait to see Ben's face as I entered the church. Madison got changed in Charlie's room, and as he walked into my bedroom, I could hear the sound of my own heart beating.
He stood for a minute, not saying a word. Then he walked towards me. Taking my hand, he said, 'You look very beautiful, Anna. The car has arrived to take us to the church.'
When the girls had set off with the children, Madison took a deep breath and said, 'Are you ready, Anna?' I looked in the mirror one last time, making sure I was prefect for Ben.
Madison and I stood at the bottom of the aisle and everyone turned to look as the organ started playing. I didn't want the traditional wedding theme. So I had chosen to have the theme *Father of The Bride* played. Everything was so beautiful. The little church pews were beautifully decorated in bows that matched our dresses - claret and white. I could see the look of love in Ben's eyes as he turned around to watch me walk towards him. He smiled so softly, as Madison gave me to him and whispered, 'You look

astonishing.' After we had exchanged our wedding vows, my *husband* removed my veil and placed a gentle kiss on my head and said 'Mrs Collins, I truly love you.'

My wedding day was perfect, and everyone had a super day. Lorraine had everything arranged to perfection, as promised. After the speeches and the meal, Ben and I led our guests into the ballroom. When everyone was seated, my husband took my hand, and He lead me over to the dance floor for our first dance. Ben held me tightly as the music played. I didn't want this day to end. All the stress and nervous feelings have led up to this, and it was amazing. It was so worth it, in every way. I was truly blessed to have such a wonderful husband.
We spent five days in Venice for our honeymoon. It was wonderful. Penny had taken a week off work to take care of Charlie. Our time in Venice was blissful, and the sights were breathtaking. Shortly after we came home, Ben had arranged for the builders to start renovations in the cottage. We moved into Penny's house, and day after day I would go and watch the builders turn a once tiny cottage into a much bigger home for our new family. Even though the cottage had been transformed, the memories of my childhood days and the echo of laughter still surrounded me, and at that moment, I knew many more years of laughter were to come.

Printed in Great Britain
by Amazon.co.uk, Ltd.,
Marston Gate.